Dr P. Porcupine PhD

Dr D. S. Dragon
with Spines PhD

Dr H. Hedgehog
PhD

WHY ARE THERE SO MANY BOOKS ABOUT BEARS?

KRISTINA STEPHENSON

Hodder
Children's
Books

In the great hallowed hall of
Mollusc College, Oxford, the most
brilliant minds in the animal kingdom
(and Trevor) had come together
to discuss, debate and generally
decide if they could answer the
Impossible Question ...

Why are there
so many books
about bears?

"Might I suggest," said William Snakespeare, who was very good with words, "that the answer lies in the name.

Bear is an excellent word for rhyming. Bear rhymes with:

hair,

scare,

beware,

take care.

It even rhymes with underwear."

Everybody nodded.

"I think we have the answer," they said.

"Stuff and nonsense!" cried Albert Swinestein,
who was exceptionally good at thinking.

"I've never heard anything quite so illogical.
Pig is a good word for rhyming too.
But there aren't nearly as many books about pigs
as there are about bears."

William Snakespeare hissed and huffed.
But the clever pig was right.

"I propose," said Albert Swinestein,
"the answer must be..."

KNOCKETY,
KNOCKETY,
KNOCK!

"Tea trolley!" said the
knockety-knocker
with a cheery little cry.

"Read the sign,"
said the animals gruffly.
"It says: DO NOT DISTURB!"

So the tea trolley went away.

"Now then, where was I?" oinked Albert Swinestein.
"Ah, yes! The Impossible Question ... I propose,"
the pig repeated, "the answer must be: SIZE!

Bears can be big.

Bears can be small.

Bears can be in the middle."

"Silly theory!" said the PhDs
(that's *Porcupines, Hedgehogs, and Dragons with Spines*).

"We come in different sizes too, but where are the books about *us*?"

"Ah, but you're prickly," piped up *Newt*on,

who was ever so good at ideas.

"Bears are *soft*.

And *that* my friends, is the answer

to the Impossible Question."

Albert Swinestein patted *Newt*on
firmly on the back.
"Brilliant theory, old chap," said the pig.
"We scientists are *never* wrong."

"Well, you are this time!" said Mary Shelley,
who knew a lot about writing.
"The answer to the Impossible Question
has nothing to with science. There are so
many bears in books because ..."

KNOCKETY, KNOCKETY, KNOCK!

"I've got some *chocolate cake* on my trolley," said the knockety-knocker. "It'll go well with a nice cup of tea."

"Read the sign!"

said the animals gruffly.

So the tea trolley went away again.

"Will you please **listen?**" said Mary Shelley, who didn't like being interrupted.

"As I was saying, the answer to the Impossible Question has nothing to do with *science*. There are so many bears in books because PEOPLE put them there.

Think about it ... bears are a lot *like* people and ...

... people are a lot *like* bears."

"**Rubbish!**" shouted the PhDs.
"People don't have fur."

"Oh, don't be difficult,"
said Mary Shelley.
"You know very
well what I mean."

"Well, if I'm not right."

"And neither am I."

"And everyone thinks I'm wrong."

"Then ...

...what *IS* the answer to
the Impossible Question?"

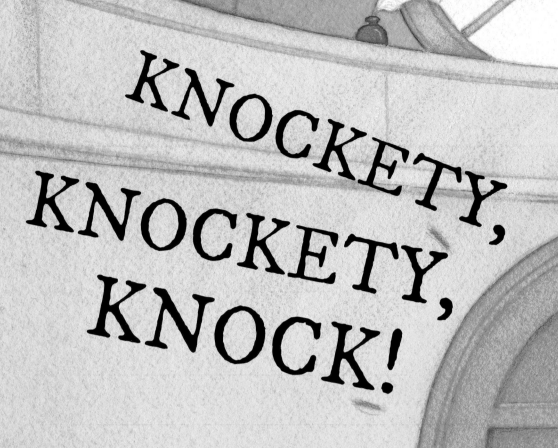

KNOCKETY, KNOCKETY, KNOCK!

"I've checked my trolley,"
said the knockety-knocker,
"and I've even got
sticky buns."

"Aaaaaaargh!"
roared the animals.

"Why won't you listen? We told you
to read the sign.
We don't want *tea.*
We don't want *cake.*
And we don't want *sticky buns.*

We just want the answer
to the Impossible Question.

So ...

...unless you have it on your trolley,

WILL YOU PLEASE

At this point, Trevor
(remember him?) dropped
the book he was reading.

"THAT'S ENOUGH!"

he shouted at the top of his tiny voice.

"There's no need to be so rude.
Might I suggest that tea and cake and
sticky buns are *precisely* what you need?
Because the answer to the Impossible
Question is right behind that door …"

In the great hallowed hall of Mollusc College, Oxford, the most brilliant minds in the animal kingdom (and Trevor) stopped discussing, stopped debating, and all had tea. Until …

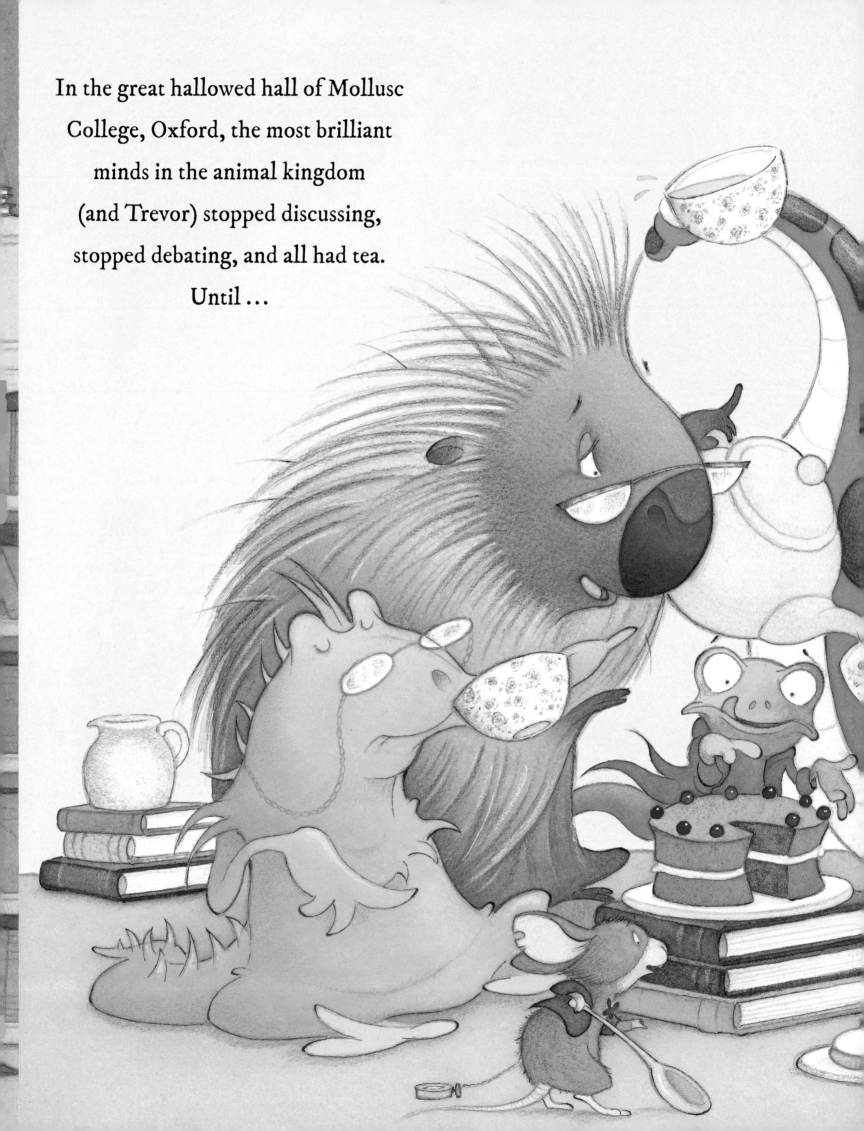

"Excuse me," said the bear,
whose name was D'Arwin.
"Could anybody tell me . . .

. . . why are there so many books about dinosaurs?"

For my friend and fellow writer, Finn Shearer,
his sister Meg, his mum Katie and his dad Richard.
With love, K.S.

HODDER CHILDREN'S BOOKS

First published in Great Britain in 2019
by Hodder and Stoughton

Text and illustration copyright ©
Kristina Stephenson, 2019

The moral rights of the author and illustrator
have been asserted.

A CIP catalogue record for this book
is available from the British Library.

HB ISBN: 978 1 444 94601 7
PB ISBN: 978 1 444 94599 7

1 3 5 7 9 10 8 6 4 2
Printed and bound in China

Hodder Children's Books, an imprint
of Hachette Children's Group,
part of Hodder and Stoughton,
Carmelite House,
50 Victoria Embankment,
London, EC4Y 0DZ

An Hachette UK Company

www.hachette.co.uk

www.hachettechildrens.co.uk

MIX
Paper from
responsible sources
FSC® C104740
www.fsc.org

Albert
Swinestein

Mary Shelley

I. Newton

William
Snakespeare